Praise for *Dangerous Men*

'In this powerful debut, Michael Katakis strips away the comfortable fabric of civilization to reveal painful truths, bone-chilling emotion, and starkly isolated souls set in a timeless winter landscape. I was reminded of Ernest Hemingway's darker stories from his own debut, *In Our Time*. Like that master, Katakis never fails to engage the reader's imagination nor evoke a strong visceral response that lingers long after the book is closed.'

CHARLES SCRIBNER III

'Michael Katakis writes well about contemporary America in these fast-paced stories that come back to haunt you like an Edward Hopper Sunday.'

PATRICK HEMINGWAY

'The stories in *Dangerous Men* are stark Western morality plays, evocative of the land and its people and the way those are ultimately mistreated. These are stories of love and violence, revenge and redemption, and of the dark, heavy sins which can never be redeemed. These stories will haunt you.'

DAVID MCCUMBER

'Michael Katakis targets the human heart with his fiction. His aim is straight and true.'

WILLIAM HJORTSBERG

'Set against the enduring landscape and depressed towns of modern-day Montana, Michael Katakis' stories are about good, hard-working people faced with immediate and life-altering decisions. He introduces his readers to emotions that conjure loneliness, to choices that mold emotions and to resolutions that cannot help but touch readers who have not fallen into the pitfall of modern-day correctness. Offsetting these extreme stories is Katakis' writing, straightforward and poetic in the genre of Jean Giono and Knut Hamsun, a difficult task he realizes effortlessly.'

GUY DE LA VALDENE

'A severe beauty of a book that uproots your own unsettling past and slays the famished ghosts. You hold your breath and vainly hush your heart as you tread gingerly down each sentence. If death can be made architectural and sublime, then Michael Katakis has accomplished just that in *Dangerous Men*.'

BELLE YANG

DANGEROUS
MEN

Also by Michael Katakis

Ernest Hemingway: Artifacts From a Life

A Thousand Shards of Glass: There is Another America

Despatches (special limited edition)

Traveller: Observations From an American in Exile

Photographs and Words (with Kris L. Hardin)

Excavating Voices: Listening to Photographs of Native Americans

The Vietnam Veterans Memorial (with Kris L. Hardin)

DANGEROUS MEN

MICHAEL KATAKIS

SCRIBNER

ONDON NEW YORK SYDNEY TORONTO NEW DELHI

First published in Great Britain by Scribner,
an imprint of Simon & Schuster UK Ltd, 2020

SCRIBNER and design are registered trademarks of The Gale Group, Inc.,
used under licence by Simon & Schuster Inc.

1 3 5 7 9 10 8 6 4 2

Simon & Schuster UK Ltd
1st Floor
222 Gray's Inn Road
London WC1X 8HB

www.simonandschuster.co.uk
www.simonandschuster.com.au
www.simonandschuster.co.in

Simon & Schuster Australia, Sydney
Simon & Schuster India, New Delhi

A CIP catalogue record for this book
is available from the British Library

Hardback ISBN: 978-1-4711-9445-0
eBook ISBN: 978-1-4711-9446-7

Typeset in Palatino by M Rules

Printed in the UK by CPI Group (UK) Ltd, Croydon, CR0 4YY

MIX
Paper from
responsible sources
FSC® C020471

For Melissa, Ian and Kris

Contents

THE FENCE

At first she nagged him a great deal ... but he
soon developed a faculty for never listening
to her. It would be impolite, he considered, to
notice her when she was not being a lady.

JOHN STEINBECK, *The Pastures of Heaven*

As the man's arthritic hands struggled to separate flesh from
wire, her dead eyes stared up at him. The horse she'd been
riding had fallen down a shallow rise, pinning them both
against the fence. As they struggled, the tangled wire worked
around the woman's neck, slowly garroting her.

He wiped the blood from the throat that years before had
demanded pearls then rested her head back on the ground.
Speaking softly, he stroked the horse's neck, took off its saddle
and let it run free. Leaning on the post, he rolled a cigarette,
looked at the mountains in the distance and down at the
initials carved into the weathered wood. They were cut years
before she had come.

Once, he had believed he could save her from the demons
that fired her rages, but found that belief was no match for

her cruelty. She understood that and took pleasure in, little by little, stripping away his self-respect, until he was nothing except a man who never objected.

Out of habit, he leaned over and studied the fence. Except for the break, he admired its straight line. The ten miles of wire that surrounded the ranch had been a part of his education. When he looked at the wire he thought of his grandfather and remembered how the old man taught him about the placement of poles, the stringing of wire and its repair. He had learned to take pride in his work, to respect other people's property and his own. The fence had given him all of that and in return he had given sixty years of his life.

In 1932, the family had fallen on hard times, forcing his father to convert the property into a dude ranch for part of the year. People came to Montana from all over the world to experience a way of life wrapped in myth and legend.

To the family's surprise, people loved it and would return with their children who, years later, would return with their own. That is how he spent his youth. He would saddle the guests' horses and guide them into the backcountry. After a day of working the wire, he'd set up camp by the Shields River.

There was a moment he always looked forward to on those outings. He'd set up camp, make a fire and feed the horses. First it would get quiet and then everyone would be looking up at the millions of stars, trying to count the shooting ones. He loved those nights because it felt like he was bringing beauty into their lives.

The beautiful girl with long, brown hair traveled to the ranch from Rhode Island in the summer of 1954, and from the time she arrived she flirted with the young cowboy. Once, while showing guests how to repair broken wire, she rubbed up behind him and looked over his shoulder. Drops of her sweat fell on his neck and when he jumped back, she, and the other guests, laughed at his embarrassment. She did that many times and took pleasure in his shock. He looked forward to the time she'd be gone, but after she left, he found that he missed her.

That is how it began. She wrote to him every week from Jamestown until she returned to the ranch. After she left, he would dream about the things they had done.

Once, after the guests had gone, she had stayed on for a few days. They rode to a place that he loved on the far east side of the ranch. In the fire's light she began to undress him and then unbuttoned her shirt and pants. That evening the young cowboy confused sex with love.

It was years later when he learned what she had done and how desperate she had been to get out of Jamestown. Back in Rhode Island she had been seeing a young painter who was starting to acquire a reputation in New York. She said she loved him and the young painter believed her. When he learned about the others, he told her it was over but, late at night, she would knock on his door and beg him to take her back. He would begin to dream again.

The back and forth became an addiction and the young man stopped painting. There was nothing but him now and he wasn't enough because she wasn't the kind of woman who cared for broken things.

Her life in Jamestown was over. She would always be known as the woman who destroyed a young man's life for no other reason than she could. She moved on, looking for another young man with dreams who would believe her.

He struggled for words as they stood naked in front of the fire.

'What do you want?' she asked.

'Marry me.'

In his arms she smiled.

'Yes. I'll marry you.'

The old cowboy looked at the straight lines of the wire and remembered the time before she had come. He had always loved the fence and in return it had provided for him. As he looked down into her dead eyes, he realized the fence had provided for him again.

HUNTER'S MOON

I could give all to Time except – except
What I myself have held ... For I am there,
And what I would not part with I have kept.

ROBERT FROST

For a long time he watched as she slept, and in the moonlight
that bathed the room he studied every curve of her. He put
his face into her thick hair, breathed deep and remembered
how they met in Paris years before. He had been a young
photojournalist covering the war in Vietnam and she an
anthropologist on holiday from West Africa.

Drinking at the Ritz, he had looked across the room and
seen her laughing with friends. Out of character, he walked
toward their table and stood there trying to speak, but stum-
bled, embarrassed by his intrusion. She simply turned and
smiled. He relaxed and introduced himself and for the rest of
the evening they talked as if they'd known each other always.
After thirty-five years they were still together.

As he stroked her hair, she opened her green eyes,
and smiled.

'Can't sleep?' she asked.

'Not when I'm next to such a beauty. It's too exciting, you know.'

'Is there anything I can do?'

He giggled like a schoolboy and his face turned red as it always did when she teased.

'I love you,' he said. 'I've always loved you.'

'Come here.'

When he woke he was alone except for Mr Bear, the big Chesapeake Bay Retriever who, for the last eleven years, had shared their lives and who loved to sneak up on the bed at night. He helped the old dog down and together they limped to the kitchen. From the window he could see her moving through the harvested rows of her garden. He began to cry, but caught himself and started preparing the scones she loved.

For three days she had no pain and it was like it had always been. After her first operation the doctors said they had gotten all of the disease but after six months the cancer returned. She endured another surgery, but again, it had returned. He remembered sitting in the stark office and how the doctor's eyes could not meet hers. He said something about statistics and another operation and described how the illness would progress. While the doctor nervously went on she looked at the photographs on the desk.

'Your children are lovely,' she said. 'You're a lucky man.'

'Thank you. That's Katy on the left and the twin boys making faces are Caleb and Michael. That's my wife Emma behind them. They're a handful. The kids, I mean.'

As was her way, she had made the doctor feel relaxed. They carried on about his family, the life she had lived in Africa and the simple things that made life sweet.

The doctor rose when she thanked him for all he had done and then expressed her wish to go home and resume the life she loved for whatever time was left.

The smell of scones greeted her as she came in from the garden. He handed her a cup of tea.

'You spoil me.'

'I'll stop it, then,' he said.

'Don't you dare.'

'How are you feeling?'

'I'm fine, dear, and I'm very much looking forward to our day.' Then she gave him the look that always drove him crazy, the look he called the 'Jezebel' face. 'And the night?' she whispered. 'I'm really looking forward to our night.'

'Don't you think we're a little old for that stuff?'

'Old?' she said. 'That must have been another man I made love with last night.'

'Did you make love with someone last night?' he joked.

She gently punched his shoulder.

'Okay, I remember. I have my moments, don't I?'

She held his face, kissed his lips and then went upstairs to finish some letters while he got out the shotguns and clothing.

Most of their life together had been lived in Montana and every fall they would go bird hunting in the Shields Valley. Over time, many of the ranches had been sold and in their places were town homes and subdivisions. In many ways it was unrecognizable from what they had known, except for their favorite place.

When they first moved to the area they were introduced to Jim Gambol. He had taken a liking to the young couple and as their friendship developed, the rancher learned that the young man loved bird hunting and offered him the use of his six hundred acres. The land was known as Gambol's field.

It had been a long time since they had first walked the foothills that surrounded the wheat fields. The Crazy Mountains
were to the east and Sumner Creek ran through the land's
center, creating an oasis of trees and wild grasses. It was
in those grasses that they had made love and watched the
Hunter's Moon as it rose above the mountains for the first
time. They had returned for every Hunter's Moon since.

By the time she came downstairs, everything was packed.
She collected the Thermos and sandwiches, while he warmed
up the car and helped Mr Bear into the back.

Driving down Brackett Creek Road, they looked over the
land that had once belonged to their neighbors, George and
Catherine Lesser. The families had shared good times but that
was all gone. The Lessers were dead and the once beautiful
hills that had been home to elk, eagle and hawk were now a
subdivision called Wild West Estates.

'Everything ends,' she whispered.

'Did you say something, dear?'

'Just talking to myself and remembering how good it's been
for us and what a grand time we've had.'

At Clyde Park he turned left and headed up Highway 89
toward Wilsall. At the power line he followed the old gravel
road past the open gate to the fence that bordered the field.
He opened her door and she kissed him as Mr Bear barked
demands for freedom. The place had this effect on them. It
was filled with their history and was a survivor in a changing
world. Like them, the field possessed grace and beauty and
very little time.

They put on their coats and pulled out the guns. For the
last six years this had been a tradition and symbolic of time
passing. Neither of them carried shells any more, they just
walked the field, guns empty, talking and remembering. It

had been a fall day like this when she shot her last bird. She never liked seeing them fall out of the sky and after the first surgery she wanted to celebrate life and not contribute to the end of things. She had insisted that he continue but he was content to walk with her and explore the world within the confines of the field.

After a short walk she became weak. He rushed to her.

'Here, let me help you.'

'You always have,' she said.

A cold wind came up as he helped her to the car.

'The weather report said that tomorrow would be clear and cold. Will we see the moon?' she asked.

'I'm sure it will be a fine afternoon, like all of them.'

'But last year we had a terrible storm and nearly froze. Remember?'

'Yes, I remember. It was a fine day because you were with me and it was fun to come home and light the fire and dance,' he said.

'Dance? Oh yes, the dance. It was fun the way you put on that old Chubby Checker record and made me twist. That was the night you pulled your back, as I recall.'

'Try to just remember the big picture rather than all the small details,' he said.

She caressed his cheek and he began to cry.

'I can't. I just can't.'

'Oh, my love. It's all right. Really. We've agreed and I'm counting on you to help me. I want it to be like now, when I'm happy. I know what I'm asking. Please.'

'Yes,' he whispered.

'And don't you dare put your back out tonight,' she whispered.

Driving home, he mentioned that he had made plans for

dinner. She had wanted to stay home but smiled when he mentioned the Mint.

By seven that evening they were driving down Bridger Canyon. The sky was clear and the stars lit up the trees and pastures. It was one of those magical Montana nights they loved. She cracked the window to take in the autumn air and then bent and turned violently, grabbing her side. Trying to help, the man nearly lost control of the car before bringing it to a skidding stop.

'It's fine, dear. I'm fine,' she said, trying to catch her breath.

'I'll take you home right away.'

'No, I'm fine, really. I want to go out tonight. I want to go.'

Over the last few days she had felt so good and had been lulled into thinking the pain had been a dream. She wouldn't think that again.

A collective cheer rose as they walked through the doors of the Mint. The man had planned the party with Jack and Karen Bender who owned the Mint. They had decided to close the place for the night so everyone could celebrate thirty years of friendship. Everyone reminisced and throughout the evening he would look across the room to wherever she was and she would sense his eyes, would turn and smile back.

People paired off and danced to the music coming from the old jukebox and for a moment they danced to the memory of a world that had once been young and had seemed for ever.

Driving home she rested her head on his shoulder.

'Tired?' he asked.

'No. I'm happy. Thank you for tonight.'

He drove on, trying not to think.

Pulling up the blinds, the morning light filled the room. She turned over and saw him standing there, holding a tray and grinning. She smelled the biscuits. The old man set the tray down and puffed up her pillows and then placed the tray over her lap. Next to the basket of biscuits was a jar of strawberry preserves from France. She picked up the jam and read the label as he moved to the other side of the bed.

'Do you remember?' he asked.

'Oh yes. I remember the Ritz and I remember how we stayed in our room for days living on eggs, champagne, croissants and this glorious jam.'

'I remember, too. It was perfect, wasn't it?'

They lay in bed talking about the years and how timing and chance had brought them together. They talked of the children they had tried for, but couldn't have, and all the miles they had traveled together. They laughed more than cried and wished for others the lives they lived. They made love and slept.

It was early afternoon when she rose. The sensation started as she walked down the stairs. At first it was nothing more than a mild spasm, but then, like a wave gaining speed, the pain crashed against her spine and she collapsed. He rushed up from the basement and held her until it passed. When she was ready, he helped her to her feet and they walked to the living room. He set her gently in the leather chair by the fireplace and then placed the old Indian blanket over her legs. With his back turned, he threw another log on the fire and quickly wiped tears from his eyes.

'How about us staying here today and enjoying the fire?' he said with his back turned.

'I don't want to miss the moon,' she said.

'There will be other moons.'

He was ashamed as the words came out, knowing they weren't true.

'I'm hungry,' she said.

'What? I'm sorry, what did you say?'

'I said I'm hungry—starving, really.'

'How about one of my omelets?'

'And champagne,' she said. 'Yes, your French omelet and champagne to celebrate.'

'Celebrate what?'

'Everything,' she said. 'Let's celebrate everything.'

Getting caught up in her enthusiasm, as he always had, he began to prepare the omelets and sliced the thick oatmeal bread while she opened a bottle of champagne.

The bread was put in a pan with butter until there was a light crust and then he covered the slices with a thin layer of strawberry jam. The omelet was placed to the side of the plate next to the halved bread. She took a bit of toast and then held it in front of his mouth. He took a bite and closed his eyes. She sipped the wine and then lifted the glass to his lips. The bubbles tickled his nose. They laughed and in that late afternoon nothing could touch them. They were in that faraway place that had always been theirs. Like Paris.

Late in the day she said she wanted to go and see the Hunter's Moon. The afternoon had been perfect and the feeling had carried him until he packed the clothing and guns and put the shotgun shells in his pocket. As always, Mr Bear sat next to him as he collected the hunting gear. The old man knelt down and hugged him as the dog licked his ear and sniffed for scents of the afternoon meal. From the stairs she watched them and felt everything that had been good in her life.

The afternoon air was crisp and the sky clear as they made their way to the field. Mr Bear jumped out while they put on their coats. He took out his gun.

'Leave mine in the car, will you, dear? I just want to walk.'

Mr Bear moved ahead, trying to get the scent of birds as they walked between the rows of wheat. Near the top of a rise she stopped, kissed him softly and then turned to look at the mountains.

He stood behind her as she watched the moon rise. Without turning she said, 'I love you.' He raised the gun and fired. Slowly she sank beneath the rolling sea of wheat. Mr Bear whined as he lay next to what had been her, and the man fired again.

For a long time he stood and watched a thin row of clouds move across the moon.

It was nearly morning when he joined them.

HOME FOR CHRISTMAS

> They did not care to question him any further
> regarding his journey, for they perceived that
> he was in a mood to go rambling all over the
> heavens ...
>
> CERVANTES, *Don Quixote*

Bill Gambol poured a cup of coffee and stared out the window
to where the tractor was stored. He remembered when his son
drove the machine and how the field's dust rose into the air,
muting the morning light.

Jimmy Gambol had been a happy boy and, like his parents, he had a strong sense of right and wrong. In school he
was the peacemaker, the boy who broke up fights and made
people laugh. Bill couldn't help but wonder if his son would
be here if he hadn't talked so much about what was right, or
the little guy. Since Jimmy had left he had been doing a lot of
second-guessing.

Given how he was raised, it was no surprise when one day
Jimmy came in from the fields and said he was volunteering
with the Red Cross in Bosnia. Over the last year, the fighting

had intensified and Jimmy had become upset at the pictures in the paper. He talked about poor kids caught up in violence and questioned why he was lucky while others were born into misery.

He spoke with the town minister and asked how God could allow such things. The preacher told him that destruction was Man's making and that Man would have to change it.

Jimmy Gambol was an idealist but his faith and sense of justice were tempered by the reality of ranch life. In his nineteen years he had known hard work and long hours. He had witnessed birth and death and learned early about the end of things.

When Jimmy was ten, Ollie, the family dog, had gotten caught in an old wire trap about half a mile from the house. The dog's leg was nearly severed when Jimmy found him.

The November afternoon grew colder. Jimmy tried to open the trap, but it wouldn't give so he took off his jacket, lay next to his friend, and covered them both.

Bill had been calling for Jimmy since 5 p.m. He looked at the sky. It was getting dark. The temperature was dropping. He telephoned the sheriff and all the neighbors he could reach.

The volunteer's boots made crunching sounds on the frozen fields and the light from their lanterns reflected the breath that rose from their mouths. It was late when they found Jimmy with his dead friend.

In the hospital, Bill told his son that Ollie was gone. The boy blamed himself.

'I tried, Papa. I really tried to get the trap open. Maybe I could have dragged him home.'

'No son, he was too heavy. You did everything you could, but it was foolish what you did.'

Jimmy looked down and began to cry.

'Yes, what you did was foolish, son, but it was one of the most unselfish things I've ever seen. Old Ollie died peaceful because his friend was with him. He just went to sleep.'

'Really?' the boy asked, wiping tears.

'Really. When that trap got Ollie I'm sure he was about as scared as anything could be. But with you there, I know he felt safe.'

'When I die, will God let Ollie and me be together?' Jimmy asked.

Bill didn't hear his wife come into the kitchen. He was still lost in thought when she walked over and topped off his cup.

'Are you sure he'll be here for Christmas?' Verna asked.

'Morning,' he said, turning to kiss her. 'Yes. They said he would be on the early flight. He's getting into England tonight and then connects with another plane.'

'I'm glad,' she said. 'He's never missed a Christmas. It wouldn't be the same.'

'No. It wouldn't.'

Bill picked up his coat, brushed her cheek and pulled her close.

'I better get to work. There's a lot to do before tomorrow.'

He walked to the door and looked back but she had already turned toward the decorated mantel filled with photographs.

Verna Gambol straightened some of the Christmas stockings and ran her fingers over the worn fabric that spelled out the children's names. She stared at the family pictures and laughed when she saw a picture of Jimmy in his Daniel Boone hat sitting on a pony. He was making one of his rubber faces. Before turning she looked at the last photograph.

Jimmy had his brother Matt on his shoulders. Katey, the youngest, stood by his side while Mary, the second oldest, stared seriously into the camera. Bill had turned a second before the picture was taken and was looking to the side laughing while Verna smiled at them all. It was a good memory.

'Morning, Mom,' said Matt as he walked into the kitchen.

'Morning. Some breakfast?'

'No thanks. Just coffee. I want to go help Dad.'

'Dress warm, it's cold now and it's going to get colder.'

'I will, Mom. Don't worry.'

Matt stood beside the old table and ran his hand across the worn surface, feeling its dents and scratches. The wine stains from Thanksgiving made him sad, somehow. He looked across the room and watched his mother filling the holiday stockings and knew nothing would ever be the same. He put down the cup and tried to remember when he had believed in things, but he couldn't remember and that made him sadder than he ever thought he could feel.

Soon, he would leave the ranch but he couldn't tell them. They had lost too much already.

'See ya at lunch, Mom.'

Katey held up her pajamas and walked over to the Christmas tree, staring at the silver angel on top.

'Is Santa bringing Jimmy?'

'Well, Katey, Santa has a lot of deliveries tonight, so Jimmy will be coming on a plane in the morning.'

'Can I sit on his shoulders?'

Verna picked up the tiny girl, tickled her stomach and began to spin around while Mary watched from the doorway. Wouldn't it be better if they all stopped and just said the words, Mary thought, but then she thought again. No, maybe it was best for everyone to live inside an illusion where they could catch their breath and pretend.

Verna and Katey were dizzy from the spinning.

'What are you crazies doing?' asked Mary.

'We're being silly and it's fun,' yelled Katey.

'Can I play?'

'Sure,' said Verna. 'Come on.'

Together they turned, slow at first, then faster, until reality blurred. They savored the moment like wine, trying to get everything from it before the feeling disappeared.

Down in the field Bill and Matt were trying to break the frozen ground with a backhoe. It was slow going but, finally, the land gave way.

'It's a good thing we made that fire last night, Dad. I don't think we could've got under without it,' said Matt.

'It was good thinking, Matt. I would have felt bad if we hadn't finished. It would have upset your mother.'

As they stared into the hole, Bill said, 'I don't believe I've ever been so cold.'

'It's the wind, Dad. It makes it colder.'

'Come on. It's Christmas Eve and your mom has been cooking all day. Only a pair of damn fools would stay out here when there's a warm fire waiting.'

Bill walked to the old Ford and Matt looked back. Like Jimmy, he was learning about the end of things, too.

The wind was blowing hard when they pulled up to the ranch house.

'Matt, by the look of that sky it's gonna get even colder tonight. We need to put the truck in the barn and plug in the heater.

'You go, Dad. I'll take care of it.'

Matt pulled the heavy cord into place and set the heater close to the truck's radiator. He wondered what it mattered if they made it on time tomorrow but suddenly caught himself. Walking out he turned into the wind until he couldn't feel his face or hands. Of course it mattered, he thought. It all matters.

The warm kitchen felt good as Matt hung up his coat. Bill and Verna were laughing at Katey who was performing her imitation of Santa Claus.

'I hope you're not making fun of Santa,' said Mary. 'He might think you don't like him and then he might not come.'

A shocked look came over Katey's face and she nearly started crying, so Matt jumped in.

'Santa knows you're joking.'

'Just teasing, sweet pea. Of course Santa is coming. Why, no little girl has been as good as you and Santa knows that,' said Mary.

'Then he'll bring Jimmy home. Because I've been good.'

Bill picked up his little girl and tussled her hair.

'I love you, Daddy.'

'I love you too, sweet pea. Now, everybody. Let's eat.'

Everyone was talking as the food made its way around the table. They talked about the past and about futures.

Katey wanted to be a doctor, and Mary hoped to be a veterinarian. Verna looked on as Bill told the children how proud of them he was. They reminisced about Jimmy's practical jokes and what a good brother he was. That night they remembered the best of him and each other and in the remembering there was grace. They believed life would go on and were assured by their faith that there were no endings. They believed all that and the believing, for a time, gave them peace.

After dinner, next to the dying fire, Bill drifted off as the world of the Gambols settled into a hushed silence. In a dream he saw Jimmy walking off the plane and waving.

'It's good to be home,' he said. 'I'll never leave again.'

The sound of sizzling pans and tearing paper woke him.

'Wake up, Papa. Wake up,' said Katey.

'I'm up, sweetie.'

'It's Christmas, Papa.'

The kitchen smelled of bacon and eggs and biscuits. Verna put on a Nat King Cole record and sang along out of key.

'Chestnuts roasting on an open fire. Jack Frost nipping at your nose.'

'When do we get Jimmy?' asked Katey.

'Around ten-thirty. We should start getting ready,' said Bill.

The sky was clear and there was no wind as they made their way down the canyon. Bill looked at the Bridger Mountains in the distance and Verna watched as a neighbor's mailbox came into view. It had always seemed to be there, though she remembered when it wasn't. It was not that long ago when the young couple moved into the area. The couple had seen their children grow, and were Mary's godparents, and Verna remembered how they had loved to watch the Hunter's Moon rise over the mountains.

They knew words. They would have found the right words, she thought, but they were gone.

Bridger Canyon seemed deserted as they made their way to Gallatin Field. The plane had arrived early and was parked at the gate. They stood by the terminal windows looking at people walking down the ramp.

Beside the plane three men were positioning a large cart. Bill watched and then, without thinking said,

'There's Jimmy. There's my boy.'

They all looked at him and then outside. Except for Katey, they had all known, but the knowing didn't help. They watched as the men unloaded the flag-draped coffin onto the cart. Verna began to cry and Mary just stood there. Matt turned and Bill couldn't help any of them because he was far away now.

Bill Gambol thought of himself as a boy and of all the Gambols who had worked the land. He thought of the deep hole that he and Matt had dug where Jimmy would be lying tonight, and then he thought of the fields that Jimmy had worked and loved.

In time his son would be one with the dust. The wind would pick up what he had been and then settle him back down across the fields, announcing, for ever, that he was home.

PART ONE:

The Final Tally of Walter Lesser

Reason will not decide at last: the sword
will decide.

ROBINSON JEFFERS,
'Contemplation of the Sword', 1938

THE DECISION

Walter Lesser sat on the bed and stared into the eyes of his
reflection in the dresser mirror. He picked up the Smith &
Wesson from the nightstand and opened the cylinder. Seeing
it was loaded, he closed it and rested the gun on his thigh.

He checked the shine on his boots, brushed some lint from
his jeans and for a second time began to rearrange the things
on the dresser.

His mother and father's wedding photograph in the tar-
nished frame was moved to the right. A silver belt buckle he
had won at a rodeo in Wyoming sat next to his grandfather's

timepiece. He moved the photograph of Mary Hollins, a girl he had courted in Montana, to the left and in the center he placed two envelopes. One was addressed to Mr Jack Wells, Deep Well Ranch, Livingston, Montana, and the other to Mrs Annette Janowski.

'That's fine,' he said to himself, 'just fine.'

Walter straightened his hair and took a drag from his cigarette. Through the smoke he looked in the mirror and admired the sharp creases in his shirt and then took a last look at the room covered in plastic sheeting.

He lifted the gun and pulled back the hammer just as his father had done in 1960. The barrel felt hard against his head. He watched himself in the mirror, oddly detached as he watched the reflection's actions that would end his life.

A day ago Walter Lesser had gotten the news but it had only begun to sink in last night. The doctor had told him about some tests, but the word 'terminal' had been pushed to the back of his brain.

Walter Lesser was not afraid to die because in many ways he had been dead for years, ever since they stole the ranch and he did nothing.

He focused on Mary's photograph and was overcome with a grief and regret that had never passed. 'My poor Mary,' he whispered. Pushing the memory aside, he readied himself again. His right forefinger squeezed the trigger but he hesitated, dangling between the worlds of here and after.

He couldn't stop the pictures flooding into his brain and began to remember happier times. Picnicking with Mary by Crooked Creek, sitting in his father's study playing chess and his mother fussing over dinner and her blue dishes.

He remembered how free he had been and the remembering

was painful. There was that time when the ranch hands gave him his nickname, Smiling Slim.

Folks had always taken to Walt. He had a smile that was inviting, and with his six-foot-three lanky frame and gentle good looks he reminded people of Gary Cooper.

The memories turned ugly. He could see his father, thin and defeated, sitting at his desk, lifting the gun to his head and firing, and then his mother finding the still-life that had been her husband. It had been too much. Two months later, her broken heart just stopped.

The memories were relentless and merciless in their clarity and detail. The picture of James Ringer flashed by, consuming Walt with rage.

James Ringer, a wealthy California developer, had conspired with four county commissioners to get the Lesser property. The idea was to divide the ten thousand-acre ranch into twenty-acre parcels. The development would be called Wild West Estates.

There would be town houses, condominiums and a golf course. The old barn would stay for effect, as would the Lesser family cemetery. 'These props,' as Ringer called them, would add an air of 'Old West' authenticity.

Ringer was interviewed in San Francisco about questionable development practices that he'd been accused of. 'I'm an artist,' he said, 'and I see the land as my canvas.'

Ringer was preparing his new art. The land would be the canvas where he would create his masterpiece. He would become richer than he already was. One detail stood in the way. The Lesser family.

Ringer tried to buy the ranch. His offer was politely declined. George Lesser had told him that the ranch was more than land. His parents and grandparents were buried there.

'This ground,' he said, 'is rich in the blood and bones of the Lesser family. We're the land, the land is us and we'll never sell what we are.'

James Ringer had heard the word 'no' before. He was a man used to getting what he wanted by any means necessary. His favorite saying, which he repeated often, was: 'Salesmanship begins when the sucker says no.'

The trouble began in the fall of 1958, when Ringer's paid thug, Russell Byers, confronted George Lesser and warned him that it might be best to sell while he could.

'Barns have been known to burn in the night,' Byers told him.

George struck Byers with an uppercut, knocking him to the ground. Getting up, he was struck again.

'I will not tolerate any threats against my family or property,' said George, as Byers cupped his bleeding nose.

Two nights later, a fire burned down the Lessers' barn and stalls. Sixteen dairy cows and twelve horses perished. The next morning George tried to press charges but the sheriff said there wasn't enough evidence to charge Byers. In spite of the protests from George's wife Catherine and some of the ranch hands, George and Walt drove into Livingston looking for Byers. They found him in the Mint Bar. Byers was sitting in the corner with some pals and watched as Walt and George walked toward them.

'Hi, boys. Can I buy you a drink?' Byers said for the benefit of all his potential witnesses.

'My barn and stalls were burned last night. We lost cows and horses. You know anything about that?'

Laughing with his friends, Byers said, 'Why boys, what would cause you to think I'd do something so low down?'

'Because you threatened to do it and got that broken nose for your trouble,' said George.

'My nose, hell. I don't hold it against you, George, no sir. I could see how you might of taken what I was joking about all wrong but no sir, I don't blame you at all and I won't be pressing any charges.' Byers was laughing. His pals joined in.

'All the same,' said Walt, ' it's quite a coincidence, don't you think?'

'What do you mean?' Byers asked.

Walt moved over to Byers, but his father cut in.

'What Walt means is you make a threat to burn my property and two days later my property burns.'

Fussing with the tape across his nose, Byers's smile disappeared.

'Like I said, George, it's a coincidence and, besides, I suspect there's a lot of folks around here with a grudge against you. I'd watch yourself. They might go after your family next.'

The threat was clear. Byers sat on the bar stool but his friends stood. George grabbed Byers and struck him down. One of Russ's laughing friends grabbed George from behind and Walt grabbed him. After knocking out the man's wind, Walt stood back and turned toward the other men and encouraged them to enjoy their drinks. Seeing their friend struggling on the floor trying to catch his breath, they took his advice.

George picked up the bleeding Byers and in front of everyone said:

'If you ever set foot on my land again, or do anything to harm my family, God help me, I'll kill you and Ringer. You tell 'em that.'

That night, in spite of them having been outnumbered four to one, the sheriff arrested George and Walt on charges of assault. There had been plenty of witnesses.

The family would learn too late that the game had been

rigged months before in California and Montana. The conspiracy was well planned. They never had a chance.

Walter was crying now. The memories were too much. He pushed the gun harder into the side of his head, hoping it would go off on its own. He wanted it all to stop but he couldn't pull the trigger. He felt frozen in place and in some perverse way forced to remember what he had been trying to forget for years. The memories bled out of every part of his brain where they had been hidden. He remembered how the county commissioners, along with Ringer, had managed to cut a development road through the Lessers' ranch, claiming the agricultural road had always been a county one. Then, when it was time to sell the Lesser cattle, it was discovered the herd had hoof and mouth.

The Lessers hired an attorney but after a year they were nearly broke. George asked the bank for an extension on his loan. He was refused. He had no way of knowing that the bank had been purchased by a surrogate of Ringer's the year before.

The final blow came when George received a letter from the county assessor's office. The letter stated that the Lessers had underpaid their taxes for the last two years. Documents had been altered to support the claim. With penalties and interest, the total owed was $13,575. Payment was due in ninety days.

With taxes due, his loan being called and the lawyer's fees, George was losing the ranch. Through tears Walt saw his father walk out to the family cemetery on the knoll that overlooked the Bridger Mountains. He placed some wildflowers on his mother's grave and then walked back to the house. In his study, George raised the gun to his head and fired.

Walt was covered in sweat and weeping as he placed the gun back on the bed. After all these years he remembered it

all. The rage ran deep. He stared at his parents' photograph.
There were accounts to be settled. They were long overdue.
He stared into the mirror and straightened his hair.

The phone rang.

'Walt, where are you? Dinner's on the table.'

Walt looked at his watch. It was 7.30 and it was Friday.
Every Friday he would have dinner with his landlady and her
ten-year-old son, Michael.

'Sorry, Annette. I lost track of time. I'll be right down.'

Walter Lesser returned the gun to the dresser drawer and
took out a piece of paper. He reminded himself that once he
had been more than a transient bookkeeper who wandered
from place to place. He was more than someone who ended up
shooting himself in a Chicago apartment. He had been a man
with a life, a good life, and now he was a man with a history
again. He began to tally the years of restless travel and then,
in a precise, neat column, he wrote seven names.

James Ringer
Russell Byers
Harry Colds
Sam McCormick
Bill Jakes
Norman Mitchell
George Lazlo

LEAVING CHICAGO

Walter walked down a flight of stairs and knocked on the door
of apartment 2B.

'Come on in.'

Annette was in the kitchen.

'I hope I didn't interrupt anything, Walt.'

'Nah Annette, I was just daydreaming and lost track of time.'

Annette Janowski was a small woman with beautiful features and short blonde hair. She was a widow. Four years ago, her husband, a roofer, had fallen to his death while on a job. Talk around Chicago was he'd been murdered over gambling debts. Since moving in, Walter had been doing Annette's books. She couldn't pay much so she lowered Walt's rent and had him over for dinner every Friday. Over the last two years they had become friends.

'Tonight I've made lamb chops in a brown sauce with asparagus and baby potatoes,' said Annette.

'And an apple pie with ice cream,' said Michael.

Walt chuckled.

'It sounds great. I think you folks are trying your best to make me a fat cowboy.'

Walter watched as Michael set the table and Annette fussed over the sauce and realized they were the only people he had gotten close to in nearly twenty years. Since leaving the ranch, he had moved eighteen times. His time in Chicago was the longest he had stayed anywhere and, for a moment, he thought leaving Chicago might be wrong. Then he remembered. He was dying.

Over dinner, Michael and Walt complimented the chef, offering up ever-grander toasts, trying to outdo each other. Walt insisted on clearing the table and doing the dishes.

'Okay,' said Annette. 'I'll dry.'

They stood by the sink in silence.

'Walt?'

He didn't hear her.

'Walt?'

'Yes, sorry, what, what did you say?'

'Are you okay?' she asked.

'Well, I, I think.'

Annette's voice broke. 'Oh, Walt, you're leaving. You're going, aren't you?'

Michael, who had been doing his homework at the kitchen table, heard what his mother said. He sat frozen, waiting for his hero to say his mother was wrong.

'Yes, I'm sorry. I'll be leaving in about a week. Don't worry, Annette, I'll have all your books in order bef—'

'Enough about books, Walt.'

'Why are you going?' Michael asked in a trembling voice.

'There's something I didn't do a long time ago that I should have. I've been running ever since. I have to face it now.'

Annette Janowski saw a look in Walter's eyes that she recognized from living in Chicago.

'Don't do anything you can't live with, Walt.'

'I'll try, Annette.'

Michael was crying. Walt leaned over and hugged the boy.

'You're my best friend, Mike, and this isn't easy, I know. You're the closest I've come to family in a long time and I'm thankful for that. I love you and I need you to be strong for me and for your mom. I really need your help.'

Michael wiped his eyes and hugged Walt hard. Walt looked over to Annette.

'Now look, you guys. The Patio Theatre is playing a Gary Cooper movie. Let's go see it.'

'You men go,' Annette said.

'Nothing doing,' answered Walt. 'Mike, you take one arm, I'll take the other.'

It was two blocks to the Patio Theatre. From a block away they could see the marquee all lit up with the big black letters spelling *High Noon*. Walt loved the movies. Over the years he had filled a lot of lonely hours sitting in darkened halls watching stories where truth and justice won in the end. In the movies everything turned out okay. Michael had never seen the picture and that excited Walt.

They ate popcorn and Milk Duds and watched Gary Cooper stand up for what was right. Near the end of the film, one of the bad guys grabbed Grace Kelly. Michael yelled, 'Look out,' then turned to Walt, embarrassed.

'I did the same darn thing the first time I saw the movie,' Walt whispered.

On the walk home, Michael couldn't stop talking.

'Why did the town turn its back on him?' he asked.

'I guess people are just afraid sometimes,' Walt answered. 'I guess they forget that not doing the right thing is what they should be scared of.'

'Have you ever been scared?' Michael asked.

'Sure, but remember Gary Cooper was afraid of those bad guys and his fear didn't stop him. He still did what he thought was right.'

Walt walked Annette and Michael to their door.

'See you tomorrow, Walt.'

'See ya, Mike.'

Annette held Walter's hand. 'I wish you'd stay.'

'You don't know how much I wish I could, Annette, but wishing won't help. I don't have much time.'

His eyes betrayed his secret.

'Oh, Walt. I'm sorry. I wish you'd stay. I could take care of you. You're a good man. I'll miss you. I'll pray for you.'

'Thanks, Annette. Thanks for everything.'

Walt lay on his bed and fell asleep to the hum of the neon sign over Nick's Diner and dreamed of open spaces.

WINNEMUCCA AND HARRY COLDS

The Reckoning

Driving out of Chicago, Walt switched on the radio and turned the dial. Patsy Cline's voice faded in and out. He opened the window, took a drag from his cigarette and settled back, lost in the music.

A few years back he heard a rumor that Harry Colds had sold his interest in the Montana ranch to Ringer and then moved to Winnemucca, Nevada. Before leaving Chicago, Walt called Nevada information. Colds was there.

Harry Colds had been a neighbor of the Lessers. While never close, the two families attended the same church and social gatherings. When Colds ran for county commissioner, he asked for George and Catherine's vote. They, along with other ranchers, voted for him and he won.

Walt's earliest memory of Colds was seeing him beat his dogs. He remembered how he seemed to enjoy it. Driving through Illinois he recalled how his father had helped Colds in 1951 when the heavy rains nearly destroyed everyone's hay. While George Lesser didn't much care for Colds, he was still a neighbor and neighbors helped each other.

In 1934, George's father and Harry's father had made a handshake agreement to cut a road through both properties. The idea was that the road would give better access to remote parts of both ranches. It would also be a short cut to town, cutting nine miles off the old route. It was agreed that they would both share in the expense and maintenance of the road and that it would only be used by the two families.

All went well until Harry's father died and Harry became commissioner. When it came time for the road's maintenance, George, Walt and some of the ranch hands pitched in. For his part, Colds sent county workers on county time to help. George told Colds that wasn't right. It was a private road, he said, and county workers had no business working on a private road. Harry told George not to worry and continued to use county workers. For a time, George kept his tongue, hoping it would pass.

Harry Colds had been friends with James Ringer and, together, they had been planning to develop the area for years. Colds had not used county workers simply because he was dishonest. He understood that his father's agreement had been agreed to with a handshake. There was no document to prove an agreement had ever been made.

By using county workers on the private road, Colds began to create a paper trail. In time, the myth being created would take on the appearance of fact.

In hindsight, it was clear that the foundation of the Lessers' destruction had been constructed by a neighbor. The success of Ringer's plan depended on Harry Colds doing his part.

In less than a year and a half, Colds had documented $40,000 of county money spent on the upkeep of the road. He signed a document stating that he had always understood from his father that the road was a county road and then had the document witnessed and notarized.

Walt had driven hard, stopping only for gas and coffee. It was late and the fatigue had set in. He checked into a cheap motel and fell asleep with his clothes on. He tried to sleep but the day's bad coffee kept pulling him back. Around 3 a.m. the pain in his neck had him sit up fast. He fell off the bed and crawled to the bathroom. He wrenched open the bottle of pills and they scattered across the floor. He grabbed three, shoved them in his mouth and lay back on the cracked tile.

At 6 a.m. he came to. The pain was gone. He heard the

crunching of pills as he tried to get up. He picked some up and put them back into the cracked plastic bottle. He showered and shaved then walked to the motel office and handed the keys to the young woman behind the counter.

'I hope you enjoyed your stay,' she said.

'Yes, thanks. Can you tell me if there's a place nearby where I can get some breakfast?'

'Sure. Just turn right out of the motel and about a half mile on your left you'll see a sign for Stella's.'

The idea came to Walt as he ate his breakfast. The thought disturbed him. He wanted to confront the men responsible but hadn't thought it through. What did he want? Did he want them to pay according to the law? No, he thought. The law had let him down before. What then? Nothing would bring back his family, so, what was it he wanted? From the moment he had put down the gun in Chicago he knew what he wanted. He wanted their lives.

He left some money on the table and walked out. The morning was clear but a cold wind had come up.

There was no wind in Winnemucca that morning. The sun was out and the town was beginning its day. The Griddle House was full of regulars – ranchers, truckers, motel owners and some card dealers from the casinos. Some of the neon signs that ran down Main Street were already on and a few of the casino's gaming tables had early action. Interstate 80 was empty except for the occasional passing rig.

Eighteen miles east of Winnemucca the land was hilly and barren. From the highway the landscape was deceptive. It gave the impression of a waterless, sun-baked soil that could produce next to nothing. But off the highway and toward the foothills there were productive fields with plenty of water.

Down a long, well-groomed road was the Double Irons

Ranch. It wasn't a working ranch; it was a rich man's ranch and had the pretences a rich man's ranch had. There were Arabian horses and a large outbuilding that was like a luxury hotel for horses. In the pasture were some llamas and sheep and three pot-bellied pigs.

The house was one level with big windows. The interior, done by Cold's dead wife, Marjorie, was understated and elegant.

They had been happy there, but without her the house was a constant reminder of what had been.

The owner rose early. Since his wife's death his sleep had been restless and, sometimes, frightening. He found that he was afraid much of the time but didn't know why. He took the blue cup and saucer from the pine cabinet and poured some coffee. Long ago the cup, with all the other blue cups and dishes, had belonged to Catherine Lesser. He had forgotten that.

For years he had pushed back a lot of memories and what he couldn't forget he had rationalized. What happened to the Lessers was not his doing, he thought. After years of telling himself that, he came to believe it was true. Besides, the family would have lost the ranch anyway. George Lesser was a bad businessman. Better that he and Ringer had gotten hold of it instead of a developer that didn't care about the land. After all, he and Ringer had brought money and jobs into the community. They had provided housing for folks. Rich ones.

In all his rationalizing he chose not to remember how he had become rich off the misery of the Lesser family. He would remind himself that he had become a deacon of his church and had done good things since those early days. He was sure his good deeds made up for the past.

He had thought about George's suicide over the years, but no rationalizations seemed to quiet the memory. He kept telling himself that George was responsible. He had choices. He could have sold when they first offered a fair price. Since Marjorie's death, George Lesser was haunting Cold's dreams.

After breakfast he went into the bathroom and stared at his reflection in the mirror. Exploring the lines on his face, he was surprised by the dark circles under his eyes and his skin's grayish color. It was as if all the evil he had done was written on his face. He closed the window. A cold wind had come up.

By 9 a.m. that night, Walt was in Winnemucca. He hadn't been there in years. He wondered if Martin Alicante, his father's Basque friend, was still there and if Martin's beautiful daughter Maria would remember him. The Alicantes had owned Martin's, a Basque hotel and restaurant, for over fifty years.

Walt drove down the old street by the railroad tracks and remembered his father telling him that the best steak anywhere was at Martin's place. He turned where memory directed and there it was. The whitewashed walls and hand-painted sign with faded black letters looked the same.

He rolled down the window and could hear the music playing inside. He was hungry, hungry for familiar faces and a good steak. Stepping through the swinging doors was like stepping back in time. Everything seemed the same, from the red vinyl bar-stools to the wine-stained tables. A young woman came up to him.

'My God. Maria,' he said.

'May I seat you, sir?' she asked.

Walt was taken up in the past. Years ago they had been the best of friends, and clumsily had learned about love in the back of his truck.

'Sir,' the young woman interrupted.

'Maria?'

'Oh, are you looking for my mother?'

Walt looked embarrassed. 'I'm sorry, yes. I'm looking for your mother.'

'She's in the back. May I ask your name?'

'Just tell her an old friend.'

The woman showed Walt to his seat and glanced back before walking behind the bar and into the kitchen. The beautiful woman with long black hair was rubbing her hands on her apron as she walked towards Walt's table. She searched her memory for some reference to the stranger. Walt stood up.

'Have I changed that much?' he asked.

Maria said nothing until her arms were around him.

'You're still my handsome cowboy.'

Maria's daughter and the locals watched as the two of them held each other.

'Let me look at you,' she said. 'Where did you go? Why didn't you come here after your family's troubles?'

'I got lost for a while.'

Maria took off her apron and ordered wine. As patrons came and went, the old friends talked through the night. Maria told him about unrealized dreams and the things that had gone well. Walt told her about his life after the ranch. Maria cried. Walt assured her that he was all right and then asked if she knew where Harry Colds lived.

'No, Walt. *No no, mi carrameo*. Move on. Better to stay with me. Revenge brings misery.'

'I have no time, Maria. I'm dying.'

Maria didn't look up. 'I remember, Walt. I remember it all. It was good. I wish . . .'

Walt was smiling. His eyes were red.

'I remember, too. It was good. I'm grateful for those days and for you.'

'Colds lives west of here, about fifteen miles. His ranch is the Double Irons.'

'Thank you, Maria.'

Maria crossed herself and turned. 'God be with you.'

Walt pulled into a truck stop for coffee and gas. It was past midnight when he drove past the Double Irons sign and up the long drive. Stopping alongside the road, he shut off the truck's lights and sat in the dark. There was no moon. He drove on until he saw some lights in the distance. Parking behind a small rise, he got out of the truck and followed the road to the house. Until some dogs began to bark.

Walt slept in his truck. He woke and poured some coffee from the dented thermos. He didn't know what he was going to do but understood that if he did do something, it was going to be bad.

Sipping coffee, he heard Maria's words and began to think she was right. Then a sensation moved from his back to his chest, paralyzing him with pain. He couldn't speak or catch his breath; he just sat there sweating and pushing against the steering wheel. And then, like an outgoing tide, the pain retreated. The times between the pain's leaving and return were growing shorter. He understood that before long the pain wouldn't leave at all.

He forgot Maria's words and hardened himself. Taking a drag from his cigarette, he got out of the truck and started up the road. A few hundred feet from the house was a barn. Inside he found some rope and an old milking stool and then waited but wasn't sure for what. Sitting behind some hay bales he watched the door.

After a few hours the door opened. Walt covered his eyes from the morning light.

A man walked over to one of the empty stalls and then turned. As Walt's eyes adjusted he could see the man. Harry Colds had changed. He had lost his hair and put on some pounds, but those dead eyes were still the same.

Colds was walking toward the door when Walt rushed him. Turning, Harry Colds felt a hard blow to his head. When he came to, Colds was sitting on a milking stool. His hands were tied behind his back and a rope was around his neck.

The barn door was closed. Dogs were barking and scratching to get in. In the dark Colds began to see the outlines of a figure standing in front of him. He concentrated on the stranger's face and when it came into focus he yelled out, 'Oh God, George.'

Then he remembered that George Lesser was dead. He was relieved, then realized it was still bad news.

'Oh, Walt,' he said, 'what are you doing? You know I was a small part of what happened. It wasn't me, Walt. Yeah, I know and can tell you the whole story.'

Walt just stared at the pleading man. Colds offered him excuses then money and said something about being forced to cooperate with Ringer and how he still had grandchildren who needed him. Walt didn't hear any of it. He was lost in thought and wondered how such a nothing of a man could have destroyed his family. Finally Colds's voice broke through.

'It was a long time ago, Walt. In my own way I've tried to make up for those days. I became a deacon in my church and, believe me, I know I will pay for my sins.'

Walt listened without expression.

'I don't know how bad it's been for you all these years, but I'm sure it's been real bad. I could make the rest of your life easy. I've got lots of mon—' Colds caught himself and realized the absurdity of his situation. Of course he had lots of money; he stole it from the family whose son was standing in front of him.

Colds panicked. 'Please, for God's sake, don't kill me.'

'Where are the others?' Walt asked.

'Ma ... McCormick and Jakes were killed in a car accident four years ago and Mitchell died of cancer last year. He died slow, Walt, yeah,' said Colds, hoping the news would get him somewhere.

'What about the others?' Walt asked as he reached into his pocket.

'Well, Ringer is still there,' said Colds.

'Where?'

'You know.'

'Where?' Walt asked again.

Colds was afraid to say. He was afraid to tell Walt what Walt already knew.

'He's living on your folks' ranch. He fixed up the old place and moved in a few months after you left. I had nothing to do with that, no sir, nothing at all.'

'What about Lazlo and Byers?'

'They're all out there. Byers is in Livingston and I think Lazlo's up north. Glasgow, I think.'

The dogs were still barking and scratching at the barn door.

'Those dogs just love me,' said Colds nervously. 'People are going to hear them carrying on and come to see what's up. You better get going while you can. I swear I won't say nothing.'

Walt stared into Colds's eyes and knew he was lying and Colds knew that he knew he was lying. No one was coming. They were alone.

'Don't kill me. Please don't.'

Walt pulled his hand out of his pocket, retrieving the hamburger he bought at the truck stop. He unwrapped it and put it on the ground between the legs of the stool.

'I'm not gonna kill ya, Harry.'

Colds's mouth shifted into a trembling smile. From one of the posts Walt untied the rope that went over the rafters and around Harry's neck. He instructed the man to stand on the stool. Crying, Colds did what he was told. Walt took up the slack and tied off the rope.

'I remember how you used to beat your dogs, Harry, and I'm betting you've done the same to those dogs out there. You probably haven't fed them for a while, either, but I could be wrong. You might be a changed man, like you say.'

As Walt walked out the dogs rushed in. Colds started talking to them in a calm voice.

'Potter, Black Boy, easy, boys, easy.' Smelling the meat, the dogs dove at the stool. Colds started yelling. The dogs sensed his fear.

'Get outta here, you son of a bitch,' Colds said, before kicking at one dog's face.

Potter, remembering his beatings, bit Colds's leg. Colds screamed just as Black Boy dove for the meat again. The dog tipped the stool, and for a moment Colds balanced the stool on two legs as the rope tightened around his neck. He was trying to say something before he choked to death.

Back at the truck, Walt threw up. He drove away but had no idea where he was going. It didn't matter because he understood that revenge was not sweet, and that he was no avenging angel. He was just a dying man who'd committed murder. Driving on, he told himself the others would be easier.

GEORGE LAZLO

A Very Cold Autumn

It was an unusually cold October. The predictions were for a hard winter.

Late autumn was Walt's favorite time of year. He loved the clean, cold air, with its bite and how it stung when he inhaled fast. Driving north he remembered his family's camping cookouts that came at the end of the busy summers.

The women would prepare a few weeks before while the men tended to the cattle and the other chores that the ranch demanded. The tradition took place in the last week of September. George, Catherine, Walt and some of the ranch hands, along with a few neighbors, would pack up supplies for three days.

After saddling the horses, Walt guided everyone to a corner of the ranch.

Once there, horses were fed and a large fire was made. The women unpacked the pots of chili and made biscuits in their camping ovens while the men pitched the canvas tents. Old Rollie, one of the ranch hands, played his fiddle and the couples danced under the evening sky that showed a million stars.

Walt rolled down the window. The cold autumn air rushed in and mingled with his memories. It was fun to play them back like an old recording. The sharp pain brought him back. He focused on the landscape, trying to get his bearings, and struggled to keep the truck under control. He swerved left, nearly crashing into an oncoming car, and then turned right into a ditch, hitting his head on the wheel.

He never lost consciousness but it took a long time for the pain to subside. His hand fiddled around in the bag and found the pills that the doctor in Chicago had given him. Dr Petrosian told Walt that in a month or so the pain would be bad and that the pills would help, at least for a while.

Walt was determined to hold off for as long as he could. He had to have his wits about him. He tossed the pills back in the bag.

George Lazlo had moved out of Park County seven years after Ringer took possession of the Lesser ranch. The *Livingston Enterprise* reported that its former county commissioner and one of Livingston's most prominent citizens was moving to a large ranch in Glasgow, Montana. The editorial went on to say that George Lazlo had done good service for the people of Park County and would be missed. The author, who, by the way, was Lazlo's cousin, also extended the county's good wishes and thanks.

What the editorial had not said was that Lazlo had been quietly encouraged by the city attorney to leave town. Lazlo always had a weakness for young girls, and while he had been a powerful commissioner he had been able to silence legal assaults with cash or threats. It was different now but even though Lazlo wasn't a commissioner any more, he knew where the dirty secrets were buried. The city attorney was well aware of that because he had gotten a lot of pressure from family values Republicans who didn't want their own transgressions known. The district attorney couldn't sweep it all under the rug because that might get the state police involved and then no one could control it. Better to keep it in the family, he thought.

The girl that Lazlo had recently introduced to womanhood was fifteen years old. She was the daughter of a newcomer from California. The city attorney knew that people in Park County didn't care much about justice and cared even less if it was an outsider, especially from California. If it had concerned a local girl, it would have been a different story. The father of the girl was a day laborer and not well off so he couldn't make too much fuss.

In the closed hearing the girl was vilified. Lazlo's defense attorney made innuendoes about prostitution and entrapment, while the prosecution offered no objections. The presiding judge found Lazlo not guilty. The girl's father was given $1,500 to go away and keep his mouth shut. The matter was closed.

Before the hearing, Lazlo had met with the district attorney and a few influential citizens. It was agreed that they would make Lazlo's mess go away under the condition that he would leave Park County. Lazlo had no choice; he took the deal.

The other matter that the Livingston paper never covered, though it was whispered about for years, was what had been done to the Lessers and by whom. Some Montanans had a strange code. Even when people knew someone was a shit they were reluctant to say so, even to friends who might unsuspectingly get involved with that person. As for outsiders, you were on your own.

Livingston, like a lot of places, was rich in rumor. The folks who didn't have the guts to say things out loud would whisper in the dark and, like most small towns, get the story wrong. In the case of Lazlo, the rumors were true. Lazlo had surpassed Ringer with his cruelty and ruthlessness. George Lazlo was a sociopath. As a commissioner he had been skilled in getting people to do what he wanted by persuasion, though he preferred threatening them.

'He liked to see the fear well up in their eyes,' a friend once said. 'For him, fear was like sex with the girls. He had all the power. They could cry and plead, but it didn't matter. Only what he wanted mattered. It was like being God.'

Unlike Harry Colds, George Lazlo had never given what he had done to the Lessers a second's thought. He had forgotten how he and Bill Jakes had altered the county assessor's records, declaring the Lessers' road a county one. For his crimes Lazlo made $1,500,000 from the Wild West Estates fraud. A portion of that money had been used to purchase a ranch in Glasgow, Montana. His wife of twenty-three years had been born and raised in that country and was eager to return. With all that space maybe he'd be different, she thought, even though she knew the beatings would continue. The abuse was as much a part of her life as her children. Yes, the children. Maybe in Glasgow they would come and visit. James, her oldest, loved the fall bird hunting and surely if James came, so would Sissy who adored her older brother. Yes, the family would be together, and they would never mention the time when James beat his father after finding him with Sissy.

She had been a good mother, she thought, and had tried to explain to James, as he was walking out with his sister, that their father didn't mean it. He'd been drunk, she said. As James was walking out he stopped and kissed his mother's cheek. He understood the years of abuse had made her simple. He told her to leave but she had nowhere to go.

Walt turned into the diner parking lot. He searched his pockets until he found the folded yellow paper. He pulled the pencil from his shirt pocket and ran a line through Harry Colds's name.

Judith Lazlo's hopes about a new life in northern Montana were short-lived. Less than two weeks after moving, George was bored and drinking hard. He would come home late and yell at her, claiming the children left because she didn't support him enough or love him enough. During one of the fights, Judith surprised herself when she found the courage and spoke back.

'The children left because you raped your daughter. They never returned because they hate you. I hate you.'

George smiled. 'They hate you too, dear. Why else would they leave you with me?'

He walked across the room and brushed her cheek with the back of his hand and then slapped it as she turned away. He punched her in the face and tore at her clothes and then bent her over the kitchen table and raped her. All the while she thought of him dead and smiled for the first time in a long while.

Walt had driven all day and most of the night. It was 2.20 a.m. when he parked by the train station in Glasgow and walked across the street to the Johnny Café. A waitress carrying two plates of hotcakes moved past him.

'Anywhere, hon,' she said.

He sat in the back corner under the flickering fluorescent light and watched the railroad men come in.

'What'll it be, hon?' she asked. The old waitress with thick pancake make-up and bright red lips was adjusting the bun on her head. 'How 'bout some coffee, hon?'

'Yes, thanks.'

Sipping his coffee Walt stared at the front door. His mind wandered back to Nevada and the look on Harry Colds's face as he pleaded for his life. Even though he'd had a hand in destroying his family, Walt took no comfort from his death. He tried to rationalize his actions but couldn't convince himself, and for a moment the thought of stopping appealed to him. Maybe he could just rent a room in Glasgow and wait for his time to come.

'More coffee?' the waitress asked.

'No thanks. Can you tell me where I might find George Lazlo?'

At the mention of Lazlo's name, the café suddenly became quiet and the expression on the woman's face changed into a cold stare.

Two men sitting at the counter turned. The big man in striped overalls stood up and walked toward Walt.

'You a friend of that son of a bitch?' asked the man.

'No, I'm not a friend. I'm just looking for him, not trouble.'

The big man leaning over the table settled down and the waitress left the check.

'Sorry, mister,' he said, 'I didn't mean to come on so strong. It's jus—'

The waitress picked up the check and cut in. 'Coffee's on me, boys. Jack here is a good man, but he's soured on this guy Lazlo,' she said, and the big man nodded in agreement. "Bout a month ago, this character comes in with his wife. She's a real polite and pretty gal who'd come into the café before. She would talk about her kids with me and the other girls, so naturally, when she came in with her fella it was nice to see her. So, I walk up to where they're sitting and I say, "Hi, Judith, how's the kids?" Well this guy Lazlo stands up, pushes me hard and grabs the pot of coffee I was holding and throws it in her face. She got burned bad but that wasn't the end of it. He started slapping and punching her. I thought he was going to kill her. Everything happened so fast. Old Jack, you see how big he is, was sitting at the counter and got to Lazlo as fast as he could. Lazlo was drunk, you could smell it. Jack tried to hold the guy, and the guy stabs Jack in the shoulder with a fork. Can you believe it? A fork. Well, Jack beat the hell out of him. It took four men to pull him off. We called the police but Judith, poor thing, refused to press charges. Now get this. Lazlo is suing Jack for assault. How's that for crazy?'

Walt stood and moved to where the big man was sitting.

'How's the shoulder?' he asked.

'Oh hell, I'm okay. Better than that poor lady, I'd guess.'

'I'm sorry for your trouble,' said Walt. 'Don't worry. I have a feeling it won't last.'

Any second thoughts Walt had had about what he was going to do disappeared. This time it would be different. No games. He would get to Lazlo, let him know who he was and then shoot him dead.

The waitress had given Walt Lazlo's address. There was no point in wasting any time. He drove north for eight miles and found the entrance to the G Bar L Ranch. He rode past and found a turnout. It was 4.10 a.m. He needed to get some sleep.

A little after 7 a.m., Walt opened his eyes and drove back to the ranch entrance and parked just outside the property. Walking up the ranch road, he took the gun from his coat and checked it. At the end of the road there was a gray house with a large porch. Seeing that no one was around, he moved quickly to one of the big windows and looked inside. Suddenly he felt a crash and fell backwards on the porch. His vision was blurred and the side of his head was covered in blood.

'You son of a bitch. Rob me, will ya?'

Walt could make out a large outline coming at him and covered his head. The ax handle came down on his shin. He screamed.

From one of the outbuildings, Lazlo had seen the man and assumed he was a thief. Lazlo laughed as he turned the stranger over, asking his name so he would know what to put on the gravestone. Walt looked up.

'I'm Walter Lesser and I've come here to kill you.'

'Well I'll be goddamned. It's been a long time, boy. How ya been?' Walter stared as Lazlo poked the ax handle into his ribs. 'I said, how ya been? How's your folks?' Lazlo asked sadistically.

'Oh ya, they're dead, ain't they? Well don't take it so hard, you're gonna see 'em soon.'

The screen door opened behind them. Judith Lazlo stood there in her apron. 'Oh, how nice,' she said, 'we have company.'

George looked at his wife with contempt as she walked in front of him. 'You stupid bitch. Get in the house.'

She smiled as she raised her right hand and quickly moved the serrated bread knife across her husband's throat. Blood flooded out of the wound, staining her face and clothes. Lazlo, on his knees, grabbed his throat and was trying to say something. Judith's expression had not changed. She looked at Walt and then back at her husband. She knelt beside him.

'Now dear,' she whispered, 'just die, won't you?'

The last thing George Lazlo saw was the madness that he had put in his wife's eyes. She wiped the dead man's brow with her blood soaked apron.

'That's right,' she said. 'It's all right now.'

Wiping the knife on her apron, Judith turned to Walter.

'How nice of you to come by. My children are coming home today so I have to clean up. I hope you'll excuse me. Please, do come again.'

Walter stared at the insane woman and knew he was damned.

GOING HOME

Walter managed to make it to the truck and drove to a motel outside of Glasgow. He inspected his head and leg. Nothing was broken but his scalp could have used some stiches. The face of Judith Lazlo was burned into his brain. He nearly panicked when he thought he might not make it back to Livingston to finish what he'd started.

The pain had become stronger and now he didn't think twice about taking the pills. He lay back on the bed. Annette Janowski's warning came back to him: 'Don't do anything you can't live with.' Too late, he thought.

Walt spent two nights at the motel trying to mend. He was fighting time. He just needed a little more. Packing his things, he glanced at the photograph of Mary Hollins and remembered how it had felt to be in love. He had always intended to marry her and then build their home on the western knoll by the creek where they had made love and talked about the future.

A few years after the troubles, he had heard that Mary had married James Ringer. Ringer had taken a liking to her after visiting her father. The Hollinses' property shared a fence line with the Lessers'. People knew what had happened to the Lessers and who had done it. They were all scared of James Ringer.

Ringer had told Gus Hollins that he intended to take over his ranch one way or another.

'I have big plans for the area,' he said, 'and your ranch is part of it.'

Gus Hollins was an alcoholic who scared easily, a weakness that Ringer knew how to take advantage of. After pushing Hollins for a few months, Ringer suggested a deal. If Gus convinced his daughter to marry him, they would combine both ranches and be rich together. The old man took the deal and pleaded with his daughter to help him and the family. He pleaded with her, saying that he didn't want to end up like George Lesser. She was the only one who could save the ranch, he told her.

The wedding was a big affair, attended by many in the community, including people who had helped destroy the Lesser family and any chance of happiness she and Walt might have had.

Mary was a reluctant lover to Ringer but he always helped her to see the light with a few slaps across the face. He liked it when she fought, so she stopped fighting. When he forced himself on her she would think of Walter and the might-have-beens, as if they were real. Those memories became her reality and she sank deep within them to a place where no one could reach her.

A year after the wedding she gave birth to a boy. It had been a difficult delivery and she was bedridden for over a month.

During her convalescence, Mary was surprised to see her husband attending to every matter concerning the child. It was the only time she had ever seen him be kind. The boy meant everything to Ringer and, like everything else in his life, he had big plans for him.

One morning, Mary Hollins woke and went into the nursery. She picked up her child, kissed his head and then laid him back into his crib. She dressed, walked to the Lesser family cemetery and laid wild flowers on George and Catherine's graves. Walking over to the large cottonwood tree, she opened the folding chair she had brought from the house. She climbed up, put the rope around her neck and stepped off the chair.

In her pocket was a note. 'Please bury me next to Catherine and George Lesser.' Ringer had his wife cremated.

Walter kissed the photograph, packed the rest of his things and began to make his way home. As the landscape became familiar, Walt settled down and remembered pieces of his past that had been buried. They were good memories that he had worked hard to forget. For so long he had thought he had to forget to survive, but now he understood that the memories had always been there, sustaining the best parts of him as he'd sleepwalked through the last twenty years. Making his way back, he was grateful for the remembering.

Pulling into Livingston, Walter got some gas and a coffee to go. He walked along the railroad tracks and looked out over the countryside. There were houses and buildings that he had never seen but it didn't matter. He was home and he would never leave again and the thought of that made him peaceful in a way he hadn't been for a long time.

Grabbing his bag from the truck, he walked over to the Murray Hotel and checked in. He took a pill, sat in the chair next to the window and watched the street below. It looked like nothing had changed. He lit a cigarette, lay back on the bed and closed his eyes. He knew this was the last week of his life.

JAMES RINGER

The Final Tally

Over the last few days, Walt drove up and down Crooked Creek Road looking up at the house-filled hills that had once been his home. His home was gone and he knew that whatever he did wouldn't change that. The people living in those houses had nothing to do with the taking of land and the destruction of his family. They had no connection to the land and moved through the barn and cemetery like they were an amusement park attraction. They knew nothing of the people who had lived, loved and died there. Only one person was left who was guilty.

The next morning Walt checked out of the motel, rolled a cigarette and got into his truck. On the passenger side were two empty gas cans. He pulled into a filling station outside of town, and the attendant offered Walt a free cup of coffee and talked about how the bird hunting wasn't the same.

'Few things are,' said Walt.

'You bet. That's for sure, mister,' the man answered.

Thanking him for the coffee, Walt drove toward the White Sulphur Springs exit. The Absaroka mountains looked beautiful in the clear autumn air.

At Clyde Park he turned left onto the gravel road toward home. He mentally went through what he was going to do. Turning up the ranch road, he drove about a hundred yards from the house and parked. Walt put the pistol in his pocket and walked over to the passenger side and picked up the gas cans.

Moving behind a row of trees, he didn't see anyone outside. Remembering how Lazlo had surprised him, Walt stopped, suspicious of the silence. Finally he walked around the house and set the gas cans beside the back door. He climbed the few steps and tuned the doorknob. It was unlocked. With his hand in his right coat pocket, he stepped slowly into the house. Down the hall he could hear a voice. Slowly, he moved through the kitchen and down the hall to the right. The voice got louder. Walter stepped into the wood-paneled study. It wasn't as simple and comfortable as his father's but the stone fireplace was as he remembered it. Behind the oak desk, James Ringer was looking down at a stack of papers and talking to himself. He didn't look like the same. His gray hair was thin and his left hand trembled.

Without looking up, Ringer said, 'I knew you'd come. I always knew.'

A cold and paralyzing fear moved through Walt's body. Ringer had been waiting for him.

'You should have learned from our first fight that I don't leave things to chance.'

From behind Walt someone spoke. 'You stupid son of a bitch. Look at me, you sorry piece of shit.'

Walt saw the smile on Ringer's face. It was the same smile he'd worn the day he took possession of the ranch. It was the look of a man who couldn't lose.

The voice from behind him was louder. 'I said turn around.'

Walt turned and recognized Russell Byers.

'Thought I was dead, huh? Did you really think you'd get us, find some kind of justice? Well, did ya? Did you all of a sudden get the guts to come back here and put things right? After all these years you're still a coward and as stupid as your old man.'

Walt stood expressionless but his eyes had turned a dead gray. For a passing moment, Byers was taken aback, and afraid.

With his back turned, Ringer said, 'Finish it, Russ.'

Byers smiled and aimed the gun at Walter's head. A shot rang out and Byers looked surprised as he stared at the smoke coming from a small hole in Walt's coat. He looked down at the small hole in his shirt and then tasted the blood in his mouth. Walt stared into the eyes of the terrified man as he fell to his knees, then flat.

Walt turned. Ringer hadn't watched. He was looking out the window.

'Get rid of him, Russ.'

Walter stood there staring at Ringer's back. The silence irritated Ringer.

Ringer turned and said, 'Damn it Russ, I said t—'

His throat tightened when he saw Walt standing there

calmly, with Byers's dead body at his feet. The two men stood there.

'Walt, I've got money, lots of money. I'll give it to you. I can get you a fine ranch. I can get you anything.'

Walt stood motionless as the man began to sob.

'Jesus Christ, Walt, don't kill me. What's the point in that? You're not a cold-blooded murderer,' Ringer said, nervously looking at Byers's dead body.

Walt pulled the gun from his pocket and aimed it at Ringer's head.

'Don't, Walt. God no, don't,' Ringer said, crying.

Walt pulled back the hammer. He was beyond hearing any pleadings. Both men heard someone come into the house. While keeping the gun on Ringer, Walt stepped to the side of the door.

'Dad, I heard something like a shot from the barn.'

The young man saw his father crying and Byers's body. Then he saw Walt, and the gun.

'What's going on? What are you doing to my father?'

Looking at the young man, Walt could see Mary's eyes. This might have been my boy, he thought.

'I'm sorry, son. This is old business between your dad and me. I'm sorry you had to see this. It's best you go now.'

'You're Walter Lesser. Your dad is the man who cheated on his taxes and lost the ranch. What does that have to do with us?'

Enraged, Walt turned toward Ringer. 'Goddamn you. Tell him the truth.'

'I, I . . .'

'Tell him, I said.'

Ringer told the boy everything, how he cheated to get the ranch and how Catherine and George Lesser had died. Walt made him tell the boy about Mary, what he had done to her and how she died. The boy, in tears, stared at his father as Ringer's eyes betrayed every dark truth.

'My God, Dad. What have you done? What about Mom? How could you do that to Mom?'

Walt felt sick. He never wanted to bring pain to this boy. Everyone was broken now. Walter looked at Ringer and lowered his gun, realizing that the truth had done more damage than any bullet ever could.

'Son, take your father and get the hell out of here.'

Sobbing, Ringer leaned on his son and walked out of the study and then outside. Walt went to the back door and retrieved the gas cans. He walked through the familiar rooms, dousing them with fuel. Though the house had been redone, he could feel the memories. In the kitchen he could see himself hugging his mother, picking her up and twirling around.

'Walter, Walt, put me down, you silly boy.'

He remembered the smell of Ivory soap on her skin.

In the study his father was beating him at chess, giving him that cagey smile that he used to make Walt laugh and break his concentration.

He left the gas cans in the study and walked back into the kitchen. He looked at the place where the long dining table had been. Everyone he had loved was sitting there. The ghosts that had brought him here were smiling. He pulled the stick from his pocket. The ghosts of those he had loved vanished as he tossed the lit match to the floor.

As the ranch house burned, Walter Lesser looked out of the kitchen window to the mountains in the distance, and remembered how it used to be.

Part Two:

Cemetery Trees

When I discover who I am, I'll be free.

RALPH ELLISON, *Invisible Man*

Hal Gustafson sat on a stool at the Wilsall bar trying to get drunk when men started yelling 'FIRE.'

'It looks like it's coming from the Ringer place,' one of them said.

'The Lesser place,' Hal snapped.

'What? What did you say, Hal?' asked the man.

'I said, the Lesser place. It's always been the Lesser place.'

'Well, Hal, sure, it used to be the Lesser place,' said the man nervously.

Hal Gustafson was a good man, but not when he drank. Growing up in Park County, people remembered the nice young man who became a dangerous one after a few drinks. Hal knew it too and that's why he hadn't had a drink in nine years, until today. People noticed and took care.

Hal was a volunteer fireman, so everyone was surprised when he just sat there ordering another drink. He didn't seem like the man they knew. The person who had returned home was a respected man who shelved his dreams to take care of his parents.

'Give me another damn drink,' he mumbled. 'Two fingers this time.'

'Hal, ain't you gonna do nothin?' asked John Dolan, a rancher.

'No. Just let the goddamn place burn,' Hal said, before downing another whisky.

'Hal, that's it. I'm cutting you off. You've had enough,' said Bill Havers, the bartender and Hal's childhood friend.

'You're right, Bill, I've had enough. I've had enough of this town and all the good and decent people. Good people, my ass. Where? Where are all the good people? The lies, Bill. Goddammit. Don't you get tired of all the lies?'

'What the hell are you talking about, and what does it have to do with the damn fire?'

'I told you. Let the goddamn place burn. Burn the whole town for all I care. It should burn, until there's nothing.'

Hal Gustafson had been a man with dreams. He'd grown up in Park County but had gotten out as fast as he could.

Like Jimmy Stewart in *It's a Wonderful Life*, Hal Gustafson dreamed of traveling the world. As a boy he wanted to be a doctor, a missionary doctor who would help people in hard places. He made it to university and was on his way when, in an instant, a phone call took everything away.

Hal's mother called and told him that his father, John 'Butch' Gustafson, had had a stroke and couldn't manage his insurance business. So began Hal Gustafson's life of frustration and regret.

Because he was a decent man he attended to his parents and the business without complaint. A few months after coming back, he joined the Park County Volunteer Fire Department. Friendships were made and the camaraderie between the men, and one woman, was a welcome diversion and an outlet for Hal's need to help others.

He had always hoped never to return, but he never knew why. The place always seemed wrong, somehow. Everything seemed shrouded in secrets but he never knew if what he was feeling was real or imagined. He remembered how after George Lesser shot himself, his own home had grown darker with something unsaid always lingering in the air.

He waded through his father's papers, hoping, when Butch got better, that he would sort all this out. Then he could leave and try again. It was wishful thinking. He knew his father wasn't coming back.

Nine months after Hal's return, Clara Gustafson, his mother, died of a heart attack, and soon after, Butch's condition worsened.

Coming home after work on a late afternoon, Hal was surprised to find his father sitting up in bed and alert.

He motioned Hal closer and in a clear voice said, 'Son, I gotta say something bad ... I need to say, I mean confess. I gotta say it before I go.'

'Going on a trip, Pop?' Hal asked, smiling.

Agitated, the old man began slurring his words.

'Knock it off. I'm going. I gotta, I just have t ...'

'What's this talk, Dad? You're looking better than I've seen you in a while.'

'No time. No goddamn time. Listen, please.'

'Okay, Pop. I'm listening.'

Butch was coughing and motioning Hal to come closer,

afraid someone might hear, even though they were alone. When his lips touched his son's ear, he whispered, 'Lesser. George and Catherine Lesser.'

Hal met his father's eyes. 'What about the Lessers?'

'They're dead. They're all dead.'

Thinking his father was having a moment, Hal smiled sympathetically. 'I know, Dad. The Lessers have been gone for a while now. You know, I think their boy—you remember Walter? I think he's still alive.'

Butch became more agitated and started to yell. 'No. Don't you see?'

'See what, Dad?'

'They're all dead. I did it. Ringer, me, the others. I killed them. We killed them. Are ya listening?'

Startled, Hal stared at Butch and thought he was delusional, but something felt dangerous, like secrets coming apart.

'Pop, what is this?' But Butch, weakened by his efforts, had drifted off.

Hal let his father sleep and then went upstairs to his parents' bedroom. As a boy he had never given much thought to the small file cabinet next to the dresser. But now, after what Butch had said, it seemed oddly out of place. He tried opening it but it was locked. He went through the dresser drawers looking for the keys, but came up empty.

The sound of breaking glass had him rush back downstairs. In the small room next to the kitchen he found Butch dead, with open eyes that followed him around the room. He touched Butch's cheek, closed the old man's eyes, and felt guilty by the flush of relief and freedom that overwhelmed him. Pulling the sheet over the body, he noticed a thin gold chain around his father's neck, and at the end of the chain, a small key.

Hal lifted his father's head and removed the chain. He

knew somehow that it would open the cabinet but was suddenly overtaken by fear. He was torn between wanting to know and terrified by what he might find.

Hal made his way upstairs and stood in the bedroom doorway, looking at the small cabinet. Kneeling down he turned the key and then sat on the floor going through Butch's ledgers and documents. They told a horrible story and revealed what he had always felt, except, now, it was real.

There were documents showing how his father had altered insurance policies so that they would not cover the Lessers' barns and stalls after Byers and his friends burned them down. He learned that Ringer's plan to steal the Lesser property was in fact his father's plan. Butch had been the architect of the entire scheme.

Hal's anger and sorrow jumbled together until he felt dizzy and lost, and just when he thought he had seen the worst, he came upon a petition for divorce by Mary Hollins against James Ringer. He recognized his father's handwriting on top of the document and on the added pages at the back. He read it all and then Hal Gustafson threw up and struggled for air, as if punched in the chest.

Mary Hollins had gone to Butch, whom she considered a friend, asking for help. She already had a lawyer in Billings, Montana, who Butch didn't know or have any leverage on. He realized that if Mary was granted an okay by the court to proceed with the divorce, lawyers would comb through Ringer's assets to determine what Mary was due. The whole scheme would come apart and he, along with the others, would be broke and in jail. Butch told Mary he would help, and then he told Ringer. He asked him to talk to Mary and convince her to hold off. 'Tell her she'll get a share,' Butch said. Ringer agreed. Four days later Mary Hollins was dead.

At the top of the petition, Butch Gustafson wrote down a date and: 'James Ringer murdered Mary Hollins.'

On the other pages he explained.

James Ringer told me he strangled his wife after she went to bed. It had to look like suicide, he said. He called me to help with the body because he was going to hang her on the old cottonwood tree next to the Lesser cemetery. I said no and he threatened my family. He said I started all this and was an accessory to murder whether I did the actual killing or not. I had no choice. I drove to Ringer's place at 1 a.m. and we put Mary in the back of my truck, along with a chair and some rope. Ringer had gotten some fresh flowers to put on Catherine Lesser's grave to suggest that Mary was depressed. He typed a brief note of apology on Mary's typewriter and left it in his son's nursery. He thought of everything. We took Mary to the place and struggled to get her up. Ringer put the rope around her neck trying to match the rope to the bruises from the strangling. Then we pulled her up to the chair, tightened the rope and kicked the chair away. We left her like that.

Hal got off the floor and tore apart his parents' bedroom. He threw their wedding photograph against the wall and then ran downstairs. He pulled back the sheet and punched his father's corpse again and again. He yanked the body off the bed and kicked it until his energy was spent. He drank everything in the house before jumping in his truck looking to look for more.

The man sitting in the Wilsall bar was someone else now. He was that dangerous man from the past, a dark, brooding stranger ready to explode.

Arnie Wilkinson, an old rancher who had been George Lesser's best friend, limped up to Hal.

'Hal, I know something is real wrong, and knowing you as I do, I guess that something is pretty bad. But Hal, the thing is, you know my ranch is close to George's, I mean Ringer's, and I'm too old to build anything up again. If that fire takes hold it will move fast in these winds and my place may not make it. I need your help, Hal? Hell, we all do.'

Hal looked at the old man's grizzly face and stared into his milky eyes. His decent self was fighting off the drink and rage, but barely.

'Goddamn it. Okay,' he said. 'Has anyone called the firehouse?'

'I did,' said Bill from behind the bar. 'Jack Popova was there and said he would call everyone. I suspect they're on their way by now.'

'Might as well call the sheriff. Unsure what we'll find,' Hal answered.

'You bet. I'm on it.'

'You men take your trucks or jump in mine. We're about five miles from the Lesser place and we need to step on it,' said Hal.

'I know I'm not much use on the front line any more, but George was my friend and I'd like to help somehow, if it's okay,' said Arnie Wilkinson.

The old rancher's decency made it impossible for Hal to say no.

'Arnie, you ride with me. Can you handle the radio to keep everyone informed after we get there?'

'I can do that.'

When they got there it was too late to save the house. The fire was so intense that there would be little left. Instead, everyone concentrated on not having the fire spread. After four hours they had managed to clear much of the vegetation around the house and contain the fire. The sheriff, Patrick Maskey, asked Hal what it looked like.

'Well, given the empty gas cans we found behind the house, and the way the fire was burning and the smoke, I'd say the fire was set on purpose.'

'Goddamn. Who the hell would do that?' asked the sheriff.

'I can think of a few people,' answered Hal. 'Pat, I need you to stick around. There's something worse than the fire. You'll need to make an arrest.'

'For the fire you mean?'

'No, for the murder of Mary Hollins.'

Pat Maskey stood there, thinking he'd misheard.

'What are you talking about, Hal? What murder? Everybody knows Mary Hollins hung herself, poor thing.'

'No, she didn't. I have proof.'

'Proof?'

'Yeah, proof. My father was in on it. He left a record. For his own protection, I guess.'

The two men approached Ringer and his son, who were sitting on a truck's tailgate. Ringer, in spite of losing his home, still had the look of someone who couldn't lose.

'Mr Ringer, we need to talk to you about the fire,' said the sheriff. 'Can you tell me what happened?'

'What happened?' asked Ringer. 'Well, I'll tell you what happened. Walt Lesser came into my house and murdered Russell Byers and then tried to murder me. That's what happened.'

The sheriff was visibly shaken. 'You mean George and Catherine's Walter?'

Before Ringer could answer, his son said, 'But he let us go, he—'

His father cut in. 'Now look sheriff, you have a murderer who came into my house, I mean what's left of my house, because of something he thought I'd done to his family. Well, sheriff, what the hell are you going to do about it?'

As Ringer went on, his son looked at him and tried to remember when he had believed his father was a good man.

'I know,' interrupted Hal.

'Know what?' asked Ringer.

'Butch left a record of what you did.'

'What the hell are you talking about, Hal?'

'You murdered your wife and my father helped you cover it up. It's over.'

The boy looked at his father but Ringer didn't look back. With all illusions gone, the son saw his father for the man he was. The boy struck him with such intensity that Ringer fell to the ground. The boy looked down at his father one last time, then turned and walked away.

The last light of day rested on the horizon and in silhouette Hal could see the outline of the tall old cottonwood and the other cemetery trees. There were no more secrets worth knowing. He was free.

Epilogue

The coroner of Park County, Montana, was informed that a charred body had been discovered in the remnants of the fire at the Ringer residence. It was later determined that the body was one Russell Byers and that he had been killed by a single gunshot to the chest. His death was ruled a homicide.

Following the official report, and eyewitness testimony, the Montana State Police contacted the FBI and put out an APB for the arrest of one Walter Lesser in connection with a series of murders across three states. He was never found.

It is rumored that somewhere in the foothills outside a small Nevada town, there's an unmarked grave of a man who reminded people of Gary Cooper.

ACKNOWLEDGEMENTS

I would like to thank my publisher, Ian Chapman, for his kindness and faith, and my editor, Chris White, whose work has made this book better.